Humpty Dumpty's Great Fall

Written by Alan Durant
Illustrated by Leah-Ellen Heming

Crabtree Publishing Company

www.crabtreebooks.com

Humpty Dumpty's Great Fall

Crabtree Publishing Company
www.crabtreebooks.com
1-800-387-7650

PMB 59051, 350 Fifth Ave.   616 Welland Ave.
59th Floor,   St. Catharines, ON
New York, NY 10118   L2M 5V6

Published by Crabtree Publishing in 2013

Series editor: Louise John
Editors: Katie Powell, Kathy Middleton
Notes to adults: Reagan Miller
Cover design: Paul Cherrill
Design: D.R.ink
Consultant: Shirley Bickler
Production coordinator and
    Prepress technician: Margaret Amy Salter
Print coordinator: Katherine Berti

Text © Alan Durant 2009
Illustration © Leah-Ellen Heming 2009

First published in
2009 by Wayland
(A division of Hachette
Children's Books)

Printed in Hong Kong/
092012/BK20120629

Library and Archives Canada
Cataloguing in Publication

CIP available at Library and Archives Canada

Library of Congress
Cataloging-in-Publication Data

CIP available at Library of Congress

Humpty Dumpty was a big bad egg.
He called himself the king of Eggtown.
But Humpty wanted to be the king
of the world outside Eggtown, too.

Outside Eggtown there was a very
high hill. At the top was a tall, crumbling
castle wall with a ladder against it.
Next to the wall was a deep well.

Each morning, children came to fetch
water from the well. They raced to see
who could get to the top of the hill first.

The winner climbed up the ladder
and stood on the wall, chanting,
"I'm the king of the castle, and
you're the dirty rascal!"

Humpty Dumpty watched and he listened.
"I'm going to be the king of the castle,"
he said to himself.

Early one morning, Humpty Dumpty waddled his way up the hill. He climbed up the ladder and sat on the wall.

Two little dicky birds flew down.
"Hello," they tweeted. "We're
Peter and Paul. Who are you?"

"I'm the king of the castle," said Humpty,
and he waved his arms. "You're the dirty
rascals!" he cried, and he frightened
the birds away. "Ha! Ha! Ha!" laughed
bad old Humpty Dumpty.

A pussycat jumped onto the wall.
"Meow," said the cat. "Who are you?"
"I'm the king of the castle," said Humpty.
"And you're the dirty rascal!"

Humpty Dumpty picked up the
pussycat and threw it into the well.
"Ha! Ha! Ha!" laughed bad old
Humpty Dumpty.

At that moment, the children arrived, racing up the hill. Jack was first, clutching his empty pail, followed closely by Jill.

Jack started to climb the ladder.
"I'm the king of the castle!" cried Humpty.
"And you're the dirty rascal!"

He kicked the ladder and down it fell
—and down Jack fell with it. Bang!

Jack bumped heads with Jill, and they both went tumbling down the hill.

"Ha! Ha! Ha!" laughed bad old Humpty Dumpty.

The king sent the Grand Old Duke
of York with his ten thousand men to
knock Humpty Dumpty off the wall.
They marched up to the top of the hill.

"I'm the king of the castle!" cried Humpty.
"And you're the dirty rascals!"
He threw stones at the king's men.

"Retreat!" ordered the Duke of York, and they all marched back down the hill again.

"Ha! Ha! Ha!" laughed bad old Humpty Dumpty.

All that day, Humpty Dumpty sat on the wall, enjoying being bad.

That night, a near-sighted, high-jumping cow and a little dog were walking up the hill with a dish and a spoon. The cow and the dog were arguing.

"I can see better than you," said the dog.
"I can jump higher than you," said the cow.

"Prove it," said the dog. "Jump over that."
He pointed to Humpty Dumpty.

The cow looked at the big round
thing. "I can jump over that moon easily,"
she said.

The cow ran up to the wall and jumped over Humpty Dumpty.

Humpty was so surprised that he toppled backward and fell off the wall. Crash! He hit the ground and smashed into pieces.

"Ha! Ha! Ha!" laughed the little dog, while the dish ran away with the spoon.

All the king's horses and all the king's men galloped back up, but they couldn't put Humpty together again. (Of course, they didn't try very hard).

"He was laughing at us," they said,
"but now the yolk's on him. Ha! ha! ha!"

The king's men caught the runaway dish and spoon.

They used the spoon to scoop Humpty Dumpty into the dish.

Then they took the scrambled egg back
to the palace for the king's breakfast.
And that was the end of bad
old Humpty Dumpty.

Notes for adults

Tadpoles: Nursery Crimes are structured for transitional and early fluent readers. The books may also be used for read-alouds or shared reading with younger children.

Tadpoles: Nursery Crimes are intended for children who are familiar with nursery rhyme characters and themes, but can also be enjoyed by anyone. Each story can be compared with the traditional rhyme, or appreciated for its own unique twist.

IF YOU ARE READING THIS BOOK WITH A CHILD, HERE ARE A FEW SUGGESTIONS:

1. Make reading fun! Choose a time to read when you and the child are relaxed and have time to share the story.

2. Before reading, invite the child to preview the book. The child can read the title, look at the illustrations, skim through the text, and make predictions as to what will happen in the story. This activity stimulates curiosity and promotes critical thinking skills.

3. During reading, encourage the child to monitor his or her understanding by asking questions to draw conclusions, making connections, and using context clues to understand unfamiliar words.

4. After reading, ask the child to review his or her predictions. Were they correct? Discuss different parts of the story, including main characters, setting, main events, the problem and solution. Challenge the child to retell the story in his or her own words to enhance comprehension.

5. Give praise! Children learn best in a positive environment.

VISIT THE LIBRARY AND CHECK OUT THESE RELATED NURSERY RHYMES AND CHILDREN'S SONGS:

Humpty Dumpty
Two Little Dickie Birds

The Grand Old Duke of York
Jack and Jill

Hey Diddle Diddle

IF YOU ENJOYED THIS BOOK, WHY NOT TRY ANOTHER TADPOLES: NURSERY CRIMES STORY?

Little Bo Peep's Missing Sheep   978-0-7787-8029-8 RLB   978-0-7787-8040-3 PB
Little Miss Muffet's Big Scare   978-0-7787-8030-4 RLB   978-0-7787-8041-0 PB
Old Mother Hubbard's Stolen Bone   978-0-7787-8031-1 RLB   978-0-7787-8042-7 PB

VISIT WWW.CRABTREEBOOKS.COM FOR OTHER CRABTREE BOOKS.